For Naomi

First U. S. edition

First published in Great Britain 1987 by Walker Books Ltd., London

Library of Congress Cataloging-in-Publication Data
Graham, Bob.
   The red woolen blanket.

   Summary: Little Julia carries her blanket everywhere
with her until one day when she outgrows it.
   [1. Blankets—Fiction] I. Title.
PZ7.G751667Re   1988   [E]   87-3036
ISBN 0-316-32310-1

Printed and bound by L.E.G.O., Vicenza, Italy

THE RED WOOLEN
BLANKET

Bob Graham

Little, Brown and Company
Boston   Toronto

Julia had her own blanket right from the start.

Julia was born in the winter. She slept in her special cot wrapped tight as a parcel.
She had a band of plastic on her wrist with her name on it.

"She's as bald as an egg," said her father,
helping himself to another chocolate.

Julia came home from the hospital with her new red blanket,
a bear, a gray woolen dog and a plastic duck.

Waiting at home for her were…

a large pair of pants with pink flowers and a beautiful blue jacket specially knitted by her grandmother.

"Isn't blue for boys?" asked her father.
"No, it doesn't really matter," said her mom.

Inside, under the red woolen blanket, Julia slept in her own basket.

Outside, snugly wrapped, she smiled in the watery winter sunshine.

Nothing worried Julia.

Julia grew. She slept in a cot and sucked and chewed the corners of her not-so-new blanket.

She rubbed the red woolen blanket gently against
her nose.

Julia's mom carried her to the shops in a pack on her back. The pack was meant to carry the shopping.

Julia liked it so much up there that the stroller was used for the shopping and the pack was used for Julia.

Then Julia was crawling and climbing.
Her blanket went with her.

It was chewed...

and screwed...

and oiled.

Some of it was left behind,

some went up the vacuum cleaner,

and some of it was walked all over.

It was there when Julia took her first step.

Sometimes Julia made her own small room with the blanket.
On the inside it was pink and cozy.

On the outside it was pink and lumpy. It scared
the dog.

Wherever Julia went her blanket went too.

In the spring,

and when it was hot;

in the autumn,

and when it rained.

Julia got bigger. Her blanket got smaller.
A sizable piece was lost under the lawnmower.

"If Julia ran off deep into a forest," said her father, "she could find her way back by the blanket threads left behind."

The day that Julia started school,

she had a little blanket not much bigger than
a postage stamp —

because no one else brought a whole blanket to school . . .

except Billy, who used his blanket
as a "Lone Avenger's" cape.

Sometime during Julia's first day at school, she lost the last threads of her blanket.

It may have been while playing in the school yard...

or having her lunch under the trees.

It could have been anywhere at all . . .
but now that she was growing up

she hardly missed it.

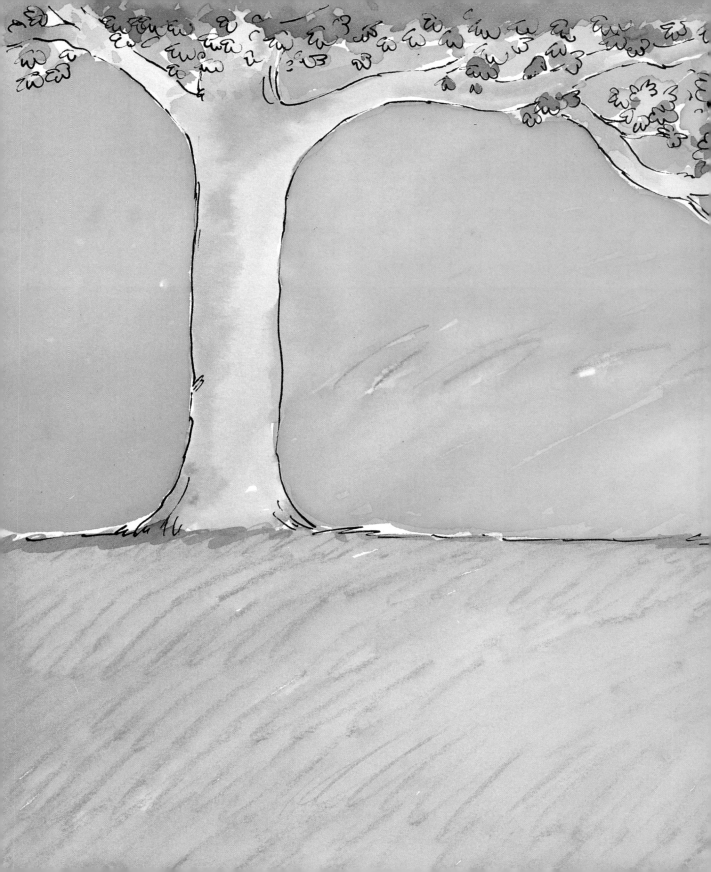